HOW CAN I HELP THE WORLD?

INSPIRING STORIES AND PRACTICAL IDEAS
TO HELP YOU JOIN IN WITH SAVING OUR PLANET

JENNY ALEXANDER

five
lanes

First published in 2019 by Five Lanes Press
Contact: info@fivelanespress.com

Contact: author@jennyalexander.co.uk
Website: www.jennyalexander.co.uk

ISBN paperback: 978-1-910300-27-5

Illustrations: Scott Garrett, www.garrettworld.co.uk
Cover and interior design: Rachel Lawston, www.lawstondesign.com
Environmental Education Consultant: Paul Lawston

---

*I would like to thank Joseph Bright, Sophie Bright, Jacob Bright,
Tegan Gerig, Daniel Gerig, Beatrice Dunn, Elizabeth Gadson,
Chelsea Hayden, Tessa Hillman, Irene Aldridge, Veronica Bright,
Chris Alton, Maria Hayden and Moira Butterfield for reading my
manuscript and giving me fantastic feedback and advice.*

CONTENTS

1
YOU CAN MAKE
A DIFFERENCE

It's amazing, the way we live today - we've got so
much stuff!

We've got crisps, fizzy drinks, ready meals, cars, buses,
trains, planes, central heating, street lighting, fridges,
freezers, dishwashers, washing machines, TV's, hair
dryers... We've got laptops, tablets and mobile phones!

Q How do dogs chat with their mates?
A On mobile bones!

The only problem with the way we live today is we're
pumping out pollution like there's no tomorrow, and it's
really harming our planet.

WHY IS POLLUTION SUCH A BIG DEAL?

Most people would rather breathe air that isn't full of fumes and eat food that isn't covered in chemicals, and absolutely nobody wants to wade around knee-deep in plastic trash.

Pollution's a pain for the individual person, but it's a massive problem for the planet.

- The earth's atmosphere is warming up.
- The ice caps are melting.
- Sea levels are rising - even huge cities like London and New York could be in trouble.
- Terrible storms, floods and wildfires are getting more common.
- Whole species of animals and plants are dying out.
- The oceans are turning into gigantic rubbish dumps.

It's pretty bad, but don't let that turn you into an eco worrier, because worriers just sit on their hands all day and do nothing.

Be an eco warrior. Get up and do something about it!

'But I'm too young!' I hear you say. Not at all. It's children and young people who are leading the way.

YOUNG ECO WARRIOR – SWEDEN
Greta Thunberg – schoolgirl activist

Swedish schoolgirl, Greta Thunberg, was only eight years old when she started to worry about climate change.
She expected the grown-up world to take action, but by the time she was fifteen things had gone on getting worse and worse, so she decided to stop waiting and do something herself.

Every Friday, she skipped school and sat outside the parliament building in Stockholm, all on her own, with a placard that said, 'School strike for the climate'.

Her protest soon got into the news, and children in other countries across the world began to make school strikes for the climate too.

What started as one girl standing up for the climate has become a worldwide student movement, and their voice is being heard. Greta has given speeches at major conferences and world leaders are listening to what she has to say.

YOUNG ECO WARRIOR - UK
Rebecca Hosking leading the way on plastic carrier bags

Twenty years ago, before anyone knew plastic was such a problem, a young film maker, Rebecca Hosking, went to make a wildlife film on Midway island, gazillions of miles from anywhere, and was amazed to find the beaches covered in plastic trash. There were loads of dead birds and animals tangled up in it, either trapped or choked from trying to eat old toothbrushes and straws.

Back home in England, she went snorkelling off her local beach and saw plastic bags drifting along the sea floor. She decided she might not be able to save Midway, but she could try and do something to help her own beach.

Rebecca persuaded all the shopkeepers in the little town of Modbury where she lived to stop using plastic carrier bags and use recyclable paper packaging instead.

So Modbury became the first plastic carrier bag free town and, as people got to hear their story, other towns soon joined in.

Because of what Rebecca started in the tiny town of Modbury, with a population of less than 2000, the UK government eventually introduced a new law in 2015 that stopped all supermarkets and large stores from giving plastic carrier bags away for free.

Since then, British people have used billions fewer plastic carrier bags each year. Quite an achievement for one young woman!

BEING AN ECO WARRIOR

Since Rebecca Hosking made her own tiny English town aware of the problem of plastic in the sea, David Attenborough has made the whole world sit up and take notice with his astonishing TV series, Blue Planet.

YOU CAN DO IT!
Get inspired

Watch Blue Planet II or, if you've already seen that one, any other film by David Attenborough – they're all amazing!

You don't have to spearhead an international youth movement like Greta Thunberg, start a local campaign like Rebecca Hosking or be a TV legend like David Attenborough with his wildlife films, to be an eco warrior.

All these people are eco warriors too:

- Seven year-old Tyler, who asked his mum to stop putting crisps in his packed lunch.
- Tyler's mum who started putting an extra sandwich in instead.
- Makayla, who saved a toad (more about that in Chapter 3!)
- 12 year-old Louis, who persuaded his school to have a blue planet day.

- Mrs Croft, who helped make it happen.
- 14 year-old Jenna who bought her backpack in a charity shop.
- Me, writing this book.
- You, reading it.

Every single one of us can make a difference.

THE STARFISH STORY

A young girl was walking along a sandy beach. Thousands of starfish had been blown ashore in a huge storm during the night, and she was throwing them back into the sea.

A man asked her, 'Why are you doing that?'

She explained that the starfish would die in the heat of the sun if they stayed washed up on the sand.

'But the beach goes on for miles, and there are millions of starfish,' said the man. 'Putting a few back in the water won't make any difference.'

The girl looked at the starfish in her hand, and threw it safely back into the waves.

'It makes a difference to this one,' she said.

The man slowly nodded his head. He started to help the girl. Soon other people joined in, until lots of people were down on the beach, all saving the starfish.

So it happened that a great many starfish were saved that day.

Being an eco warrior means making lots of little changes, because little things add up, and the brilliant thing is that when you change some of the things you do, that will soon make people around you think about their choices too.

Giant oak trees out of little acorns grow!

YOU CAN DO IT!
Make a promise

Search online for a list of the most endangered animals. Choose one.

Use a photo of your animal as wallpaper on your tablet or phone, or draw a picture of it and stick it on your wall. Give it a name. Make it a promise that you will do everything you can to nurture nature.

Every time you see it, you'll remember to think green.

2

KNOWLEDGE IS POWER!

Everything starts with awareness. If you don't know there's a problem, you can't start to do something about it. If you do know, you can. That's why they say...

KNOWLEDGE IS POWER!

Imagine if a family threw all their rubbish out the upstairs windows at the back of their house, but only ever looked out the front windows and used the front door.

No one would notice the rubbish piling up in the garden, killing the grass and flowers and making all the birds, insects and little animals that lived there homeless.

Just because no one was noticing wouldn't mean it wasn't happening. In fact, as long as no one noticed, the problem could go on getting worse.

How aware are you?

9

QUIZ: HOW AWARE ARE YOU?

Does it matter if animals become extinct?

a. No. We've got gazillions of species and we don't need them all.
b. No. The only endangered species round here is our dog when she poos on the carpet!
c. Yes, and politicians ought to do more to protect them.
d. Yes, so I did a sponsored run for the World Wide Fund for Nature.

Is plastic really that much of a problem?

a. No. It all gets buried in landfill.
b. No. There's not much litter in my road.
c. Yes, and someone should clear it up.
d. Yes. I don't buy drinks in plastic bottles.

Is global warming a bad thing?

a. Are you mad? Everyone loves warm weather!
b. It's bad if you live somewhere that's already hot, but I don't.
c. Yes, because the ice caps are melting and sea levels are rising and there's going to be more and more storms and floods, and we're all doomed!
d. Yes. I turn my bedroom light off when I'm not in there.

Does deforestation matter?

a. Nah. Who needs trees?
b. Not really – there aren't many trees where I live anyway.
c. Yes, but what am I supposed to do about it?
d. Yes. I helped with my school's tree-planting day.

TURN OVER TO FIND OUT YOUR RESULTS!

RESULTS

Mostly A...

You're as aware as an ostrich with its head in the sand.

OSTRICH FACT Ostriches don't actually bury their heads in the sand because if they did they couldn't breathe! They only look as if they're burying their heads sometimes, because they lay their eggs in holes in the ground and, several times a day, the mum puts her head down the hole to turn them over.

Mostly B...

You're as aware as a rhino – rhinos can never spot a problem because they can't see anything beyond the end of their nose.

RHINO FACT Rhinos are so short sighted that they can't tell the difference between a person and a tree more than five metres from their face.

12

Mostly C...

You know there's a problem but you don't know what to do about it. You're like a rabbit in headlights.

RABBIT FACT When a rabbit senses danger, it doesn't run away or turn and fight, it freezes. This probably works better for it in a big field where it's hard to spot than on a road when it's lit up by headlights.

Mostly D...

You're like a stalking tiger. You haven't only got the problem in your sights, you're pouncing on it!

Q What's big and stripy and goes up and down?
A A tiger in a lift!

14

INFORMATION IS MOTIVATION

Once you've recognised there's a problem, the next thing to do is get as much information about it as you can, because the more you understand the problem, the easier it is to see how you can be part of the solution.

There's loads more information coming up in this book – so keep reading!

But first, a word of warning...

When you learn about the big problems the planet is facing and discover you can make a difference, you might feel you have to do every single thing you can to help – don't go overboard.

Small changes are easy to keep up. If you try to do too much all at once, you're much more likely to give up and go back to your old ways.

You also might want everyone else to go green too, but don't badger them because, unless you've got world class powers of persuasion, you could just end up annoying them. Tell them what you're doing and why you're doing it, then let them decide all on their own whether they want to join in.

There are loads of amazing living things you pass by every day without even noticing. The bark of those trees on the pavement in your road or the roots pushing up through the tarmac... A flower, a robin, a cloud, next door's cat.

Stop and look. Take some photos. Taking photos is a great way of noticing the things you usually look straight past.

3

LOOK AFTER THE LITTLE ANIMALS

It's hard to look after endangered tigers and gorillas if you live somewhere like Norway or New Zealand, where there haven't ever been any tigers and gorillas.

Q **What do you call a gorilla with a cabbage in each ear?**
A **Anything you like. He can't hear you!**

But there are plenty of little animals right here amongst us, wherever we live, that need looking after too. We may not be down to the last three toads or the last pair of ladybirds in the world, but their numbers are dropping very fast.

Most of the little animals, such as flying insects, bats

and birds in our environment are under pressure. Does that really matter? Yes! We need our little animals, and we need loads of them.

For example, where would we be without bees?

BEES ARE THE BEE'S KNEES!

When it comes to the most important species, bees are right at the top of the list (that's what the expression 'the bee's knees' means – if you're 'the bee's knees' you're the best!)

If it wasn't for bees busy pollinating our food crops all over the world, those crops could die out. Then we'd be looking at food shortages and famines.

And it isn't only us humans that would go hungry, either. If we lost the plants bees pollinate, we could also lose the animals that eat those plants, then the animals that eat those animals and so on, up the food chain, to the biggest animals at the top.

FOOD CHAIN FACTS

1. The food chain is like any other chain – it's all linked together, and if one link breaks, the whole thing falls apart. That's why even the smallest animals matter.
2. All living things need food. Plants make their own food, with the help of sunlight, oxygen and water, so they're called producers.

Bees are in trouble across the globe, with one in ten of Europe's wild bee species actually facing extinction.

Climate change caused by the way we live is one of the pressures on bees. Here are some others:

- Farmers and gardeners are using more and more chemicals to kill pests and weeds.
- There are fewer flower meadows and hedgerows because of modern farming practices.
- Countryside is lost as towns and cities keep growing.

A WORD ABOUT WEEDS

Weeds are just plants that spring up naturally in places where human beings don't want them to grow. That's the difference between a nettle, a dandelion or a buttercup and your grandpa's prize-winning roses.

You might not be able to change farming methods or reverse climate change; you might not be able to stop your neighbours from paving over their garden or persuade your grandpa not to spray his roses, but you can make a difference.

19

YOU CAN DO IT!
Grow some bee friendly wildflowers

Get a packet of wildflower seeds. Bees love wildflowers and they're easy to grow. Also, once they get started they'll come back every year.

Follow the sowing instructions on the back. If you've got a garden, either at home or at school, see if you can have a small patch of that, about the size of a dustbin lid.

Dig up any plants that are growing in it, because your seeds will grow better if you sow them on bare earth.

If you can't find a patch of garden, a pot or window box will do just fine.

YOU CAN DO IT!
Make a watering place for bees

You will need a small, shallow dish – if your mum or dad can't give you anything suitable, you'll find one for a few pence in any charity shop.

Fill your dish with pebbles.

Pour water in around the pebbles, not deep enough to cover them, so that there are lots of tiny puddles that bees can reach to drink without falling in.

Added bonus: This makes a fine watering place for ladybirds, butterflies and other flying insects too.

SEVEN KINDS OF SMALL ANIMAL YOU CAN HELP

If you've got a garden, that's the obvious place to start. But if you haven't, think about all the places you go that do have a garden, such as your grandparents', friends' or child minder's houses, or your school.

If you ask to look after the little animals in someone else's garden, you'll be raising their awareness too. Win, win!

1 INSECTS

Bees are the champions among pollinators, but other flying insects do a lot of pollinating too. Butterflies, moths, wasps, flies, midges, mosquitos, beetles – they all spread pollen from flower to flower in their quest for nectar, and many of them are under threat.

> ### MIDGE FACT
> It's hard to love a midge, but without midges there would be no chocolate. True story! Midges are the only known pollinators of the tiny, white flowers of the cacao tree, where coca beans come from.

21

YOU CAN DO IT!
Build a bug hotel

You can build a simple bug hotel by getting a bunch of short hollow pieces of bamboo or dried out plant stems and sticks, tying them together in two places with string and posting the bundle into a hedge or hanging it in a sheltered place.

If you'd like to make something bigger and more intricate, you can bunch together some hollow tubes such as bits of drainpipe or old plastic bottles with the tops and bottoms cut off and stuff them with different natural materials like dry leaves, stones or straw.

Try one with tree bark for ladybirds, spiders and centipedes, one with rotting wood for beetles and other wood-boring insects and one with dried out hollow plant stems for woodlice, beetles and spiders.

2 SPIDERS

It's hard to love a midge, but many people would say it's even harder to love a spider! That isn't really fair because most spiders are harmless to humans and, what's more, they eat flies and mosquitos that nobody wants in their house and greenflies and caterpillars that nobody wants in their garden. They also protect farmers' crops by eating insect pests without damaging the environment like chemical pesticides do.

Having said that, there are some very, very dangerous spiders in some parts of the world, so find out whether you've got any poisonous ones in your country before you get too up close and friendly.

GIZELA'S STORY

Gizela was terrified of spiders, especially the big black ones with goggly eyes that came into her house every year in September time. If she saw one, she screamed her head off until one of her parents came and bashed it with a shoe.

But then Gizela's little bro, Henryk, did a project on spiders at school. He learnt how awesome spiders are and the next time Gizela let out one of her ear-piercing spider shrieks, he dashed up to her room and got there first.

'Kill it!' screamed Gizela.

'Noooooooooo!' Henryk screamed even louder.

The spider kept completely still, in astonishment.

Their mum came in, brandishing her slipper, but she couldn't kill the spider or Henryk would bawl his head off. On the other hand, she couldn't leave it there or Gizela would go on screaming the house down.

Their mum got a piece of cardboard from the recycling bag and a big glass from the kitchen. She carefully placed the glass over the spider, making sure not to squash any of its eight little feet.

Then she slid the cardboard underneath the glass, flipped it over and took the spider out to the garden shed.

'From now on, this is how we'll deal with spiders,' she said. Gizela said no way was she ever going to get near enough to a spider to actually catch it, so Henryk became the spider saver in their house.

But one day, when Gizela saw a spider in the hallway and no one else was around, she plucked up her courage

Famous TV gardener Alan Titchmarsh says spiders are good for the garden. 'If you meet our old friend the house spider in your bath, rehouse it in the shed. It'll be happy out there catching flies and your house will stay shriek-free.'

By the way, in case you're wondering – spiders aren't insects. Insects have six legs, but spiders have eight.

Q How does a spider find things out?
A On the web!

3 FROGS, TOADS AND NEWTS

Frogs and newts are mostly found in ponds, but toads don't need to be immersed in water so often, they just need somewhere cool and damp, like an old stone wall or a shady patch of ground.

Toads eat slugs, snails and insects and are food themselves for larger animals. But they have very thin skin, like frogs, and that makes them vulnerable to chemical pesticides and insecticides.

MAKAYLA'S STORY

Makayla's family kept their recycling bags outside in the garden shed, and it was her job to put them in the wheelbarrow and take them round the side of the house to the front once a week, when the collection lorry came.

One day, when she was picking up the glass recycling bag, she suddenly noticed a fat toad sitting among the cold, damp bottles and jars. She nearly dropped the bag in fright!

Makayla had never been so close to a toad, and she wasn't sure what she thought about it. She looked at the toad and the toad looked at her.

'You've got to go now,' Makayla said. The toad didn't move.

Makayla didn't want to touch the toad but, on the other hand, she didn't want him to get recycled either. She reached out her hand very slowly, hoping the toad would just hop away, but it still didn't move.

There was nothing for it. Makayla slowly put one hand flat in front of the toad and gently nudged him onto it. He felt cold and damp like the bottles. 'My skin must feel really hot to you,' she said.

She carried him carefully to the edge of the garden and put him in the deep shade under some bushes. Then she took the recycling out – checking there weren't any more toads in it first. When she came back, he was still there.

'If you're going to stay for a while,' she said, 'I might make you a secret watering hole!'

YOU CAN DO IT!
Make a secret watering hole

Most little animals like frogs and toads stay safe by hiding, so when you put water out for them it's best to place it in the cover of plants and bushes.

Hollow out the soil under some foliage and place a shallow dish in it. Fill the dish with water, putting some stones around the edge and in the middle, if it's big.

A few big stones and old tiles nearby could make a nice cool, damp place for frogs and toads to shelter in.

As well as toads coming to take a dip, hedgehogs may sometimes call by for a drink.

4 GASTROPODS

'Gastropods' is the fancy name for slugs and snails. Gardeners don't like them at all, because they eat all their flowers and vegetables but on the other hand, thrushes, hedgehogs and toads like nothing better than a nice juicy gastropod for dinner.

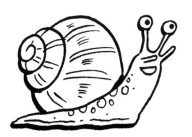

Q How do snails get their shells so shiny?
A With snail polish!

The most common way that gardeners control slugs is by poisoning them with slug pellets, but that method doesn't only kill the slugs. The poison they've eaten can go on to poison the animals that eat them.

YOU CAN DO IT!
Save a slug

Does your mum/dad/carer/gran/grandpa use slug pellets to protect their seedlings and young plants? If so, ask if you can try something else.

Slugs move by gliding along and, as their underside is soft and sensitive, they don't like crossing sharp or irritating surfaces. If you spread a good layer of sand, gravel, broken eggshells, wood ash, soot or pine needles around young plants, starting close to the stem and spreading out all around* the slugs won't like it and they'll go somewhere else.

If it works, you won't only be saving the slug from eating poisoned pellets but also any animals that might have eaten him.

* A narrow ring round the plant won't be enough because slugs can travel underground and come up inside it.

5 EARTHWORMS

On organic farms, you can find 450 earthworms per square metre of field, but in the same area of intensively farmed land you would only find 30, according to the World Wide Fund for Nature.

That's a gigantic difference.

And earthworms aren't only up against it because of modern farming methods – they're affected by global warming too, because hot, dry weather makes the soil hard for them to burrow through.

If there are too few worms, it has a knock-on effect for us in rainy weather. Earthworms make the soil porous like a sponge. If there aren't enough earthworms, the surface isn't broken up, the water can't soak away and that can lead to floods.

Charles Darwin studied worms for 39 years, and he decided life on earth would be impossible without them, because they make the soil more fertile and clear away waste.

EARTHWORM FACT

A worm can eat half its body weight in waste each day.

THE WORLD WORM CHARMING CHAMPIONSHIPS

Seriously – it's a thing! The Championships are held at Willaston County Primary School in England every year.

In 2009, 10 year-old Sophie Smith coaxed 567 worms out of her allocated square of grass.

Animals such as seagulls and wood turtles, do worm charming too. They tap with their feet, just as champion human worm charmers tap with sticks, to bring the earthworms up to the surface.

YOU CAN DO IT!
Make a wormery

- First, get a large, clean glass jar. Put a layer of sand in the bottom, about 1cm deep. Add a thick layer of soil, then another thin layer of sand, then a thick layer of soil and a thin layer of sand, till it reaches about 5cm from the top.
- Add some worms.
- Put a few old leaves on top, with some vegetable peelings, tea leaves and scraps of fruit.
- Put the lid on, but get your mum or dad to make some holes in it first because worms need air. Put some black paper around the jar and place it in a cool, dark cupboard.
- After a few weeks, take it out again and see what the worms have been up to. Earthworms speed up the process of turning scraps into compost. Your wormery might inspire your mum/dad/carer/grandparents/school to start a big worm bin outside.

6 BIRDS

Some bird species are thriving, but lots of others are struggling now, even though they were really common a few years ago.

Some birds eat fruits or berries, and spread the seeds for new plants to grow in different places when they drop them or poo them out. Seeds that hit the ground covered in bird poo grow really well - they come covered in manure!

Q Why do birds fly South in Winter?
A It's too far to walk.

Some birds eat insects, slugs, worms and snails, and they themselves can make a tasty snack for a fox or weasel.

But birds aren't only important for the environment – they're wonderful creatures for us to watch and enjoy.

When you put food and water out for birds, you get a chance to see them too, because unlike small creeping creatures that stay safe by hiding, birds need open space to spot when cats and foxes are around, so they can fly away.

YOU CAN DO IT!
Feed the birds

You can buy fatballs or feeders for peanuts or seeds, and hang them from branches or special stands, even in the smallest garden. If you haven't got a garden, you can get feeding trays that stick on the outside of your window, but if you do that, you'll want to put some pictures or stickers on the glass as well, so that the birds don't crash into it.

Here are some other bird feeding tips:

- Choose a spot where there's no cover for predators to hide.
- Feed the birds all year round, and get into a routine, so they know when you'll be putting food out for them.
- Small amounts of breadcrumbs, cooked potatoes (not chips) and breakfast cereals are fine, but they are low in nutrition, so birds need other kinds of food as well.
- Crushed, unsalted peanuts, with or without their shells are good.
- In the wintertime, birds need fats, such as mild cheese, suet and lard, but soft spreads such as margarine and cooking fats like turkey grease are very bad for them.
- Never put anything out for them that's salty.
- Clear up any leftover food on the ground or you could end up with rats.
- Wash your bird feeders thoroughly from time to time, to protect birds from catching diseases.

By the way, don't spit your chewing gum out on the ground. Besides the obvious fact that it's a yucky thing to do, birds think chewed up gum looks just like breadcrumbs and they can die if they try to eat it.

YOU CAN DO IT!
Make a bird bath

Birds don't just need water for drinking – they need it for bathing, especially in the wintertime. Bathing helps them to keep their feathers in tip top condition because the water loosens the dirt and makes the feathers easier to preen.

When they preen, birds rearrange their feathers and spread oil from the preen gland so they stay waterproof and trap a layer of insulating air underneath.

A large shallow dish or upturned dustbin lid would make a great birdbath. Put it in a place where the birds can see all around and larger animals can't creep up on them. Fill it with water and, if it's big enough, add a large stone or two in the middle for the birds to stand on while they're bathing.

7 SMALL MAMMALS

Mammals are warm-blooded animals that feed their young on milk – like us. You'll hardly ever see most of the little mammals that live in your neighbourhood – unless you've got a cat, when they might turn up dead on your doorstep.

They include rats and mice, which you really don't want to encourage, and you don't need to either, because these aren't at all endangered. Rats and mice can multiply very quickly and that means, before you know it, you can get completely overrun by them.

RAT FACT

One pair of brown rats can produce as many as 2,000 babies in a year!

How do they manage that? Rats mature quickly, so in no time at all the first litter of babies is old enough to have babies, then those babies are soon old enough to have babies, and so it goes on.

Unlike rats and mice, other small mammals are in trouble – for example, bats, which are protected by law in many countries because their numbers are falling. Bats are important because they're the only pollinators of some plants and they eat insects that can be harmful to crops.

You might see bats flying low on a summer evening, catching moths and flies or, if you're very lucky, you might notice some hanging upside down asleep in an old shed or dead tree in the daytime.

Notice them, but don't disturb them.

YOU CAN DO IT!
Put up some bat boxes

You'll need some help with this, so ask your mum/dad/grandpa/grandma/teacher.

You might have seen bird boxes nailed onto tree trunks or fixed to walls – they are basically little houses for birds.

Bat boxes are the same except they have the entrance hole at the bottom, rather than on the front, and the wood inside the box is grooved so that the bats have something to cling on to. You can buy them online or in garden centres.

Put the boxes as high as possible off the ground and, if you have more than one, place them in groups round three sides of a tree - bats like to move from one box to another during the day and from season to season as temperatures change.

If you live in Europe, Asia or Africa there's a very sweet and harmless little animal that may need your help - the humble hedgehog.

ECO WARRIOR
Michel Birkenwald – hedgehog hero!

Hedgehogs need to be able to roam over a wide area, to forage for food and find mates, but garden walls and fences make it hard for them to get about. So Michel Birkenwald, started offering a free hole-making service for all his neighbours in South London.

If anyone wants a hedgehog size hole made in their garden fence or wall, Michel and his friends will come round, drill a hole and put a little plaque up above it saying, 'Hedgehog Highway. Please keep this hole open!'

Now, the charity Hedgehog Street are trying to persuade fencing companies to supply some panels with hedgehog holes already cut in them, for people who don't have a hedgehog hero like Michel living nearby.

YOU CAN DO IT!
Become a hedgehog champion

Visit www.hedgehogstreet.org to find loads of fun facts about hedgehogs and become a hedgehog champion – nearly 50,000 people have signed up already.

Then get practical! If you have a garden, check whether there are places where hedgehogs can get through to neighbouring gardens. If there aren't, ask your mum or dad to help you find the best way of making some.

If you don't have a garden, are there places you visit that do – such as your grandparents' or friends' houses? Check if hedgehogs could move freely through and, if not, talk to them about hedgehog highways – they might not have heard about them. If your school has a garden or playing field, check that too.

YOU CAN DO IT!
Make a hedgehog shelter

Put a wooden box under a pile of sticks and leaves in a quiet corner. It's as easy as that!

38

You can do a search online to find out which particular small animals are struggling to survive in your part of the world. But wherever you are, letting nature do its thing is the best way to help them all.

YOU CAN DO IT!
Let nature do its thing

Ask your mum, dad, grandparents or anyone you know who's got a garden if they could leave a corner of the lawn to grow wild, or not mow right up to the edges. Ask your teachers the same, if your school has a green space or playing field.

A patch of long grass and wild flowers makes a wonderful home for insects, spiders, toads and hedgehogs, and offers rich pickings for birds that eat creepy crawlies and seeds.

4
CUT YOUR
PLASTIC FOOTPRINT

Plastic's fantastic! It's light, flexible, cheap and easy to manufacture. All the advances we've made in technology, transport, medicine and most other areas of our lives wouldn't have been possible without it. Just imagine if we still had to make everything out of metal, stone and wood.

But there are three BIG problems with plastic:

1. It's made from fossil fuels, using up 8% of the world's oil production.

2. It has to be manufactured and that process releases greenhouse gases and toxic chemicals into the atmosphere.

3. It breaks down, over many years, but doesn't biodegrade – which means that although the pieces get smaller and smaller, it never goes away.

For all these reasons, we should be careful how much plastic we make but we've become so enthusiastic about plastic that we've made more of it in the last ten years than in the whole of the last century.

We use plastic in ways we don't need to at all, such as adding plastic micro beads to toothpaste, face washes and cleaning products. Plastic micro beads can't be filtered out in sewage system because they're absolutely tiny, so every single one of them will end up in the oceans.

Q What comes after a sea-horse?
A A dee-horse!

YOU CAN DO IT!
Beat the micro bead

When plastic micro beads were first invented, manufacturers flashed them up on their packaging as the most wonderful latest thing, but now it's become clear what a catastrophe they are for the environment, they've mostly gone off the front of packaging and got buried in the small print on the back.

Even there, you won't see them listed as plastic micro beads they'll be called PET, PP or PMMA.

Your parents might be choosing stuff that's full of micro beads without even know they're doing it but they're probably too busy to check the ingredients in their toiletries, toothpaste and cleaning products.

You can do it for them, by either looking at the packaging or seeing if they're on the list at www. beatthemicrobead.org

We make plastic products that are designed to only be used once and then thrown away, such as drinks bottles, food packaging, plastic straws, disposable cutlery and cups, and takeaway food trays.

43

YOU CAN DO IT!
Spot your single-use plastic

For one whole day, notice all the single-use plastic that you and the people around you get through. Before you go to bed, think back and jot down everything you remember. Every single piece of that plastic could end up killing an animal somewhere in the world.

It's not rocket science, but just to be clear: 'Single-use' means it's designed to be used once and thrown away – for example, drinks bottles, crisp packets, food packaging, polystyrene pizza trays, takeaway cups...

YOU CAN DO IT!
Cut down on snack packs

Crisps, nuts, cookies... almost all our snacks are individually wrapped in plastic. It's much better for the environment if we buy big packs and pour individual portions into little re-usable food boxes.

Better still, how about sometimes choosing a piece of fruit, or making yourself a sandwich if you need to top up between meals?

You could try this delicious recipe invented by Mrs Beeton, who wrote the most famous cookbook ever, in 1861. (Yes, this is a real thing!)

The toast sandwich.

Take one slice of toast. Sprinkle it on both sides with salt and pepper. Place it between two slices of bread, and eat it. Doesn't that sound yummy?!

PLASTIC FACT

Half of all the plastic we make is designed to be used once and thrown away.

All this is building up to a huge pollution problem. Do the true or false quiz and see if you know how huge.

PLASTIC POLLUTION - TRUE OR FALSE?

1. 90% of the seabirds in the world have plastics in their stomachs. T ▓ F ▓
2. More than 90% of Americans over the age of six have a plastic chemical called BPA in their body. T ▓ F ▓
3. Every day, eight million pieces of plastic pollution find their way into the sea. T ▓ F ▓
4. A single plastic drinks bottle can break down into so many particles that you might find one on every mile of every beach around the world. T ▓ F ▓
5. 100,000 marine mammals and turtles are killed by plastic rubbish every year T ▓ F ▓
6. In the UK, a family of four throws away nearly 3,000 plastic items a year. T ▓ F ▓
7. 46% of plastic debris floats. T ▓ F ▓
8. There are vast floating islands in the oceans made completely of plastic. T ▓ F ▓
9. The North Pacific trash island is already twice the size of France, and growing fast. T ▓ F ▓
10. Plastic pollution can now be found on every beach in the world, from busy tourist beaches to uninhabited, tropical islands. T ▓ F ▓

ANSWERS

Numbers 1-3 are true. Numbers 4 to 7 are true. Let's face it they're all true! Read back over the statements and see if you notice anything about them.

Most of these ten statements are about the oceans and waterways, because that's where most of our plastic pollution finishes up.

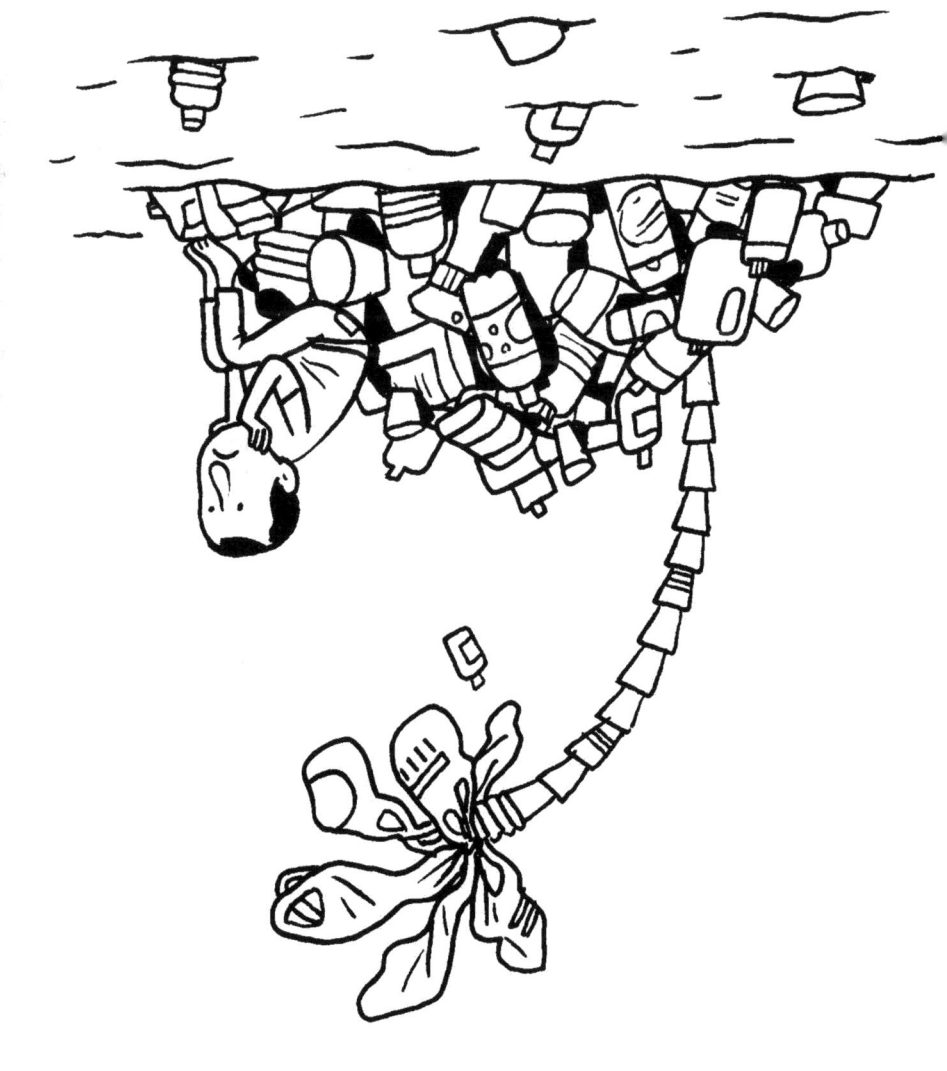

TRASH ISLANDS FACT

These islands made of plastic aren't exactly islands, but more like a vast, thick plastic soup. It has been estimated that it would take 6,700 ships a whole year to clean up the Great Pacific Garbage Patch.

Q What is a sea-monster's favourite meal?
A Fish and ships

YOU CAN DO IT!
Don't flush your rubbish down the toilet

7% of the plastic litter that washes onto our shores has been flushed down the toilet.

Here are some examples – yes, really!
- mobile phones
- toys
- disposable nappies
- cotton buds
- torches
- wigs and false eyelashes
- disposable wipes
- dental floss
- chewing gum

You might think that little things like, dental floss and chewing gum don't matter, but sea creatures can easily choke on them.

Wees, poos and toilet paper are the only things that should go down the loo.

NOTE: All tissue paper isn't made the same. Toilet rolls are designed to break down in water, but kitchen roll and tissues are designed to hold together, so don't flush them!

We can see a lot of our plastic pollution, littering our streets or washing up on our beaches, but particles that aren't visible to the human eye have also been found in the air we breathe, the water we drink and the food we eat.

We're only just beginning to wonder what kind of long-term health effects all this plastic in our environment might be having on us, in our bodies.

CHANGE IS COMING!

The first step in every positive change is recognising there's a problem, and people all over the world have started to do that.

GOVERNMENTS...

- Lots of countries worldwide have introduced bans on plastic carrier bags - in Morocco, for example, nearly everyone has switched to fabric ones.
- France will be the first country in the world to introduce a ban on all single use plastic cutlery, cups

and plates. Only those that are made of materials that can be composted at home will be allowed.

- Costa Rica will be the first country to ban **ALL** single use plastic, including plastic bottles, and many other countries, such as India, are following their lead.

BUSINESSES...

- A refund scheme on plastic bottles has made it possible for Norway to recycle 96% of its single use plastic bottles. This means less new plastic has to be made and less used plastic ends up in the ocean. Deposit return schemes have boosted collection and recycling rates of plastic bottles to over 80% in many other parts of Europe.
- Many food business and railway stations are planning to provide water fountains for people to refill their own water bottles.
- Saltwater Brewery in the US has developed a new kind of 6-pack ring that's made from wheat and barley. This means it doesn't only decompose over time, but animals can safely eat it.

ORDINARY PEOPLE...

- Many families are going back to buying washing powder in cardboard boxes instead of pre-wrapped capsules in a plastic tub.
- The vast majority of parents say they

would choose a brand that was committed to cutting down on plastic.

- One in five families have given up liquid hand-wash and shower gels in plastic dispensers and now buy bar soap instead. Some people are switching to shampoo bars as well.

We ordinary people tend to think that only governments have the power to make big changes, but the power lies with us. If ordinary people stop buying goods with single-use plastic, businesses can't sell them.

If businesses can't sell things that include single use plastics, they'll have to start supplying products that people want to buy instead.

YOU CAN DO IT!
Don't buy bottled water

Water is good for you but, in developed countries, the best water comes from the tap because it's fresh and flowing – it hasn't been sitting around in plastic for years gently soaking up the chemicals. Some plastic bottles contain the harmful chemical BPA, which can get into the water, especially if the bottles have been exposed to very warm conditions, such as in the car on a sunny day.

Besides some plastic bottles leaching chemicals, 90% of bottled water has recently been found to contain tiny plastic particles.

Re-using a plastic water bottle is better for the planet, but the best thing for you is to get a stainless steel re-useable one.

At lunchtime, your school canteen should provide cups of water, and in the UK every café or restaurant has to give tap water absolutely free of charge – a lot of people don't know that!

That's another great thing about giving up bottled water – it saves you money

NOTE: What I mean is, don't buy bottled water unless you have to. Obviously if it's a heat wave and you've got lost miles away from home and your throat is so parched you can barely speak, you may have to make an exception!

ANOTHER NOTE: Bottled water is a better choice than bottled fizzy drinks.

YOU CAN DO IT!
Don't buy fizzy drinks in plastic bottles either

Bottled fizzy drinks create all the same environmental problems as bottled water - which is funny when you think about their advertising. Fizzy drinks adverts almost always show people enjoying their drinks on perfect sandy beaches or green spaces, with not a scrap of plastic litter anywhere to be seen.

NOTE: Fizzy drinks are basically made of chemicals and water, plus either a bucket-load of sugar or artificial sweeteners that may be just as harmful to your health.

YOUNG ECO WARRIOR - TURKEY
Elif Bilgin - making plastic from banana skins

Sixteen-year old Elif Bilgin's worries about climate change led her to study different ways of making plastic, from plant material instead of fossil fuels. She learnt that bio-plastic could be made from potato and mango peelings and thought, why not banana skins then? She knew that Thailand alone threw away 200 tons of banana peelings every day.

For a couple of years, she couldn't find a method that worked, but she stuck at it, and her discovery won her the 2013 Science in Action award.

CLEARING UP THE MESS

We can all do our bit by buying less single use plastic but there will always be some plastic trash. So here's another thing we can do - clear up our mess.

All over the world, as people become more aware of the big plastic problem we've got, they're starting to clear up litter.

56

YOUNG ECO WARRIOR – UK
Elizabeth Gadsdon – little litter hero.

When Elizabeth Gadson was six, she saw a man throwing rubbish out of his car window. She felt really upset, and couldn't understand why anyone would do such a thing.

She decided to do a litter pick on the road where she lived, hoping that anyone who saw her would think a bit harder about their own actions, and stop throwing litter.

But it worked even better than that, because when people saw what she was doing, they wanted to do something too. Soon Elizabeth got lots of other people joining in with picking up litter in their streets and parks.

Some rangers from a big local park asked her to help set up a 'little collector crew' and now the crew get together once a month to do a litter pick followed by fun outdoor activities run by one of the park rangers.

Elizabeth has been recognized as a Litter Hero by Keep Britain Tidy.

You can see some videos of Elizabeth in action on her facebook page @littlecollectorcrew

Here's what she says there about her litter-picking mission.

13 MAY 2017

My name is Elizabeth and I am 8. I have 3 main missions!

- ♥ To help keep the roads and beaches near my home as litter free as I can.
- ♥ To work with my 'Little Collector Crew' and encourage them to keep places they love clean. I have helped the staff at Birkenhead Park by creating a 'Little Collector Crew' there to show everyone that children really care about our world... it is ours to look after.
- ♥ To learn more about recycling, to reduce my family's household litter, avoid plastic, never use single use plastic and educate other people.

Together we can make a difference.

YOU CAN DO IT!
Pick up a bit of plastic litter

Even if you only manage one crisp packet or plastic bottle, when you're nearly home or nearly at school so you can quickly find a bin – that's better than nothing. If you did it once a day, that's seven pieces in a week.

If you decide to do a longer litter pick, check with your mum or dad, get some protective gloves or a litter picker, don't stray into places where traffic might be a danger, and don't pick up hazardous objects like broken glass or needles. It's just common sense!

Another way that people are picking up litter in their neighbourhoods is called 'plogging.' The name comes from the Swedish for picking up trash, which is apparently 'plocka upp' (I can't swear to that because I don't speak Swedish).

Anyway, it means picking up rubbish while jogging. Ploggers carry a plastic bag when they go out running, and pick up bits of litter they see along the way. That means as well as a good run, they're also getting a full body workout, with all that bending, squatting and stretching.

It's a win-win for the plogger and the environment too!

ECO WARRIOR
David Sedaris – funny writer and champion plogger.

David Sedaris is an American who lives in the UK. He writes funny stories and, in his spare time, takes up to 60,000 steps a day in pursuit of local rubbish. He's been so effective in keeping his neighbourhood clean that the local authority has named a trash cart in his honour.

Imagine that – seeing your name emblazoned across the side of the lorry when it comes down your road collecting all the bin bags!

Plogging seems to have started in Sweden, but joggers in lots of countries are catching on to it. The Keep America Beautiful organisation is promoting it, and some areas have developed their own version – in Tennessee they call it 'trashercize.'

Whether it's walking or jogging, everyone can pick up litter. It doesn't matter how old or young you are.

Being young doesn't mean you can't have amazing new ideas about how to tidy up our mess as well, like the schoolboy inventor, Boyan Slat.

YOUNG ECO WARRIOR - NETHERLANDS
Boyan Slat - Dutch schoolboy inventor.

Boyan Slat was still at secondary school when he went on a diving trip to Greece and found himself surrounded by more plastic bags than fish. He realised that 'environmental issues are really the biggest problem my generation will face.'

Boyan had heard about giant garbage patches in the world's oceans, and he wanted to know what people were doing to clean them up. He discovered that most of the ideas being tried used nets to filter the plastic out of the water, but those nets also scooped up a lot of fish, turtles and other sea life, so he wanted to think of a better solution.

There was no time to waste. As Boyan says, 'What will happen over the next few decades is that these large objects will start breaking down into these small and dangerous micro plastics... unless we clean it up. We must defuse this ticking time-bomb.'

The idea Boyan came up with was to make huge solar powered booms that would act like beaches, sitting on the surface of the sea, gradually gathering plastic waste. Once every month or so, a boat would go and collect the garbage, just like picking it up off the beach.

While his friends were going off to university, Boyan was busy getting sponsors to help him test his invention and, six years after that diving trip in Greece, Boyan's Ocean Cleanup was ready to launch.

Inventors, ploggers and litter pickers are all doing their bit – and so can you.

YOU CAN DO IT!
Get motivated

Search online images for animals killed by plastic trash. I should warn you, some of them are upsetting – but then it's an upsetting problem.

A litter picker told me it was seeing a picture of a dead turtle tangled up in plastic that made her decide she had to get out and do something.

Everyone on the planet can be part of the solution to the plastic pollution problem, by using less and cleaning up the mess. That's called 'cutting your plastic footprint' because it means treading more carefully and lightly instead of trampling all over the planet and destroying everything.

5

CUT YOUR OTHER FOOTPRINT TOO!

You've got two feet so it makes sense that you've got two footprints! The other one, besides plastic, is called your carbon footprint.

This one isn't as easy to see as a plastic bottle washed up on a tropical beach or a plastic bag choking a turtle, but it's every bit as harmful to the planet.

Your carbon footprint is how much the way you live contributes to climate change.

Q What's the difference between weather and climate?
A You can't weather a tree but you can climate!

WHAT IS CLIMATE CHANGE?

The earth is heating up – that's why another name for climate change is 'global warming.' The reason it's heating up is because the way we live these days creates lots of air pollution, which builds up in the earth's atmosphere and traps heat, like the glass in a greenhouse.

There are several so-called greenhouse gases, including methane and nitrous oxide, but the biggest one by far is carbon dioxide. So we bunch them all together and just call them our carbon footprint.

'Our carbon dioxide, methane, nitrous oxide and other greenhouse gases footprint' doesn't quite have the same ring to it!

You might say, 'What's the big deal? It would be great if the world warmed up a bit!' But climate change is a really massive problem.

WHY IS CLIMATE CHANGE A PROBLEM?

1 MELTING ICE CAPS

It isn't only the ice at the North and South poles that is melting. There are huge ice fields and glaciers in other parts of the world, such as Switzerland, Indonesia and Peru, and they're all melting too.

All that melt-water ends up in the oceans, so sea levels are rising.

Q **What do you call an igloo without a toilet?**
A **An ig!**

2 RISING SEA LEVELS

Besides the ice caps melting, more heat in the atmosphere means the oceans are getting warmer, and warm water expands – that's science! And that's another reason why sea levels are rising.

Because of this, more than a hundred million people in coastal areas around the world could lose their homes, and even big cities like Shanghai, London, Bangkok, Jakarta, Tokyo, and New York could one day disappear beneath the waves.

YOUNG ECO WARRIOR – INDONESIA
Adeline Tiffanie Suana

Adeline Tiffanie Suana was twelve years old when she started worrying about natural disasters, especially flooding. Learning that mangroves could help limit the damage done by flooding, she set up an organisation called Sahabat Alam, which means 'Friends of Nature'.

Adeline manages groups of students who are planting mangrove trees and coral reefs and doing environmental clean ups. She has spoken at major conferences and, with government backing, presented her ideas in schools.

3 OCEAN DEAD ZONES

Warmer water holds less oxygen but, as the oceans become warmer, sea plants and animals actually need more oxygen in order to survive, not less.

In some large lakes and oceans, there is so little oxygen now that nothing can live there at all.

DEAD ZONES FACT

Global warming isn't the only cause of ocean dead zones; pollution from farming is another major cause.

4 EXTREME WEATHER

More heat and moisture in the atmosphere means more storms and hurricanes. Sudden, heavy rainfall is becoming more common, but so are longer periods with no rain at all.

So while some areas of the Earth are seeing more intense flooding, others are suffering severe droughts and wildfires.

5 LOSS OF HABITATS

Floods and droughts mean whole areas that used to support plants and animals are wiped out, but the general warming of the planet means every part of the natural world is changing, and many animal and plant species may not be able to adapt fast enough to survive.

LOSS OF HABITATS FACT

As with the ocean dead zones, global warming isn't the only problem. Modern farming is another major cause.

6 HARM TO HUMAN HEALTH

It's obvious that if you're caught up in a flood or wildfire that might affect your health! So might water shortages and heat waves.

But air pollution generally is causing health problems such as asthma and lung disease.

In terms of our mental health too, seeing our beaches knee-deep in garbage and sucking in lungfuls of exhaust fumes tends to make us feel sad.

WORDSEARCH: SPOT YOUR CARBON FOOTPRINT!

Some people used to argue that there was no such thing as climate change caused by human beings trampling the planet, because our carbon footprint isn't easy to spot. Can you spot ten aspects of climate change hidden in this wordsearch?

CLUE: They all go left to right or top to bottom.

J	I	P	A	E	X	U	E	S
E	C	D	R	O	U	G	H	T
Y	E	E	C	D	S	K	A	O
U	C	A	R	B	O	N	B	R
N	A	D	A	L	B	M	I	M
I	P	Z	F	I	R	E	T	A
F	L	O	O	D	K	L	A	M
H	B	N	D	W	L	T	T	O
M	S	E	A	L	E	V	E	L

LUCKILY, THERE'S A LOT WE CAN DO ABOUT IT!

The effects of climate change are frightening, but if we look at the causes we can see lots of ways we can all start cutting our carbon footprint right away.

The three biggest causes of global warming are power generation, transportation and farming.

POWER GENERATION

Making electricity from fossil fuels like coal, gas and oil is the main cause of climate change, according to most scientists. It's not surprising when you think of all the things we use electricity for, in our homes, factories, hospitals, shops and schools.

YOU CAN DO IT!
Turn off the lights when no one's in the room

This is so simple, and once you start doing it, it soon gets to be a habit. You could begin with your own bedroom light.

TIP: Make sure there really is no one in the room. You don't want to become an endangered species yourself!

YOU CAN DO IT!

Cut the time you spend in the shower

You don't need to soap yourself all over from head to toe every day, or take your music in the bathroom with you and sing in the steam.

Most days it's OK to just wash your face and smelly bits, which means you can be in and out of there in a jiffy!

ADDED BONUS: Not covering yourself in soap every day is better for your skin.

YOU CAN DO IT!
Switch off at the plug

When your phone is fully charged, disconnect it from the charger and turn the plug off at the wall.

If you have a computer, switch it off and unplug it when you aren't using it – don't just leave it snoozing. Electrical goods still use electricity when they're left on stand-by.

Check out how many things in your house are generally on stand-by – that'll include anything that has a lit-up panel, such as the clock on your microwave or cooker, and anything that has a remote. You might be surprised.

If there are any that are rarely used, ask your parents if you can switch them off and unplug them. (I wouldn't advise you to go ahead and do that without asking, in case you upset some complicated settings!)

TRANSPORTATION

This is partly about you and me jumping in the car or on the bus to get around, and all those people who fly off on holiday to exotic destinations.

YOU CAN DO IT!
Think about other ways to get to school

Lots of children are driven to school by car, even though many of them would have the choice of going by train or bus and nearly half say they would rather walk or cycle.

Your parents might have safety concerns about you walking or cycling to school or going by public transport, but maybe they'd be happier if you found a friend to go with or took a course on safe cycling. Or maybe you could cut your carbon footprint by car sharing with another family.

But transportation is a factor in everything we manufacture. The raw materials have to be transported to the factories and then the manufactured goods transported to the shops.

Besides manufactured goods, anything that comes from far away, such as fruits and vegetables that don't grow locally will also need transportation.

Q: Which has the lowest carbon footprint, an apple or a coconut?

A: It depends where you're eating it! In the UK, probably the apple, but underneath a palm tree in Hawaii, that would be the coconut.

FARMING

Larger fields mean smaller hedgerows. Spraying fields with chemicals means a whole industrial process to produce and transport the chemicals and then tractors and crop spraying planes to spread them on the fields.

Animal farming is the worst, because as well as the land that has to be cleared for the animals to live on, it takes a lot of land to grow crops such as soy to feed them.

YOU CAN DO IT!
Be a bit more veggie

There should always be veggie options in school lunches – if your school doesn't have them, make some noise!

You might not always have a choice at home because your mum or dad won't want to cook different dinners for you. But when you do have a choice, choose meat free sometimes. It can be as simple as having the pizza without the pepperoni.

And there's more!

I hate to break this to you, but when it comes to one of the other main greenhouse gases, methane, the cuddly cow is a bit of a villain.

Cows' farts and burps puff methane out into the atmosphere at an astonishing rate. About 27% of the methane produced by human activities comes from one end or the other of cows and other farm animals.

Although there's less methane in the atmosphere than carbon dioxide, it's a worry because it's 30 times more efficient at trapping the sun's heat. In 2010, the United Nations proposed a worldwide tax on livestock methane emissions, which the papers called 'the fart tax.'

COW FACT

Cows, like sheep and goats, have four stomachs. No wonder they produce so much gas!

COW PAT FACT

Cows' poos are full of nitrogen, and give off nitrous oxide, which is another greenhouse gas.

Q What do you get if you sit under a cow?
A A pat on the head!

THE RIPPLE EFFECT

When Greta Thunberg first sat outside the Swedish parliament with her placard, she wasn't trying to start a global student strike, and when Rebecca Hosking asked local shopkeepers to use paper bags instead of plastic ones, she wasn't expecting it to lead on to new laws across the nation.

That's called the ripple effect, like when you throw a stone into water. It makes a tiny break in the surface, but the ripples spread right out across the whole pond.

Every little thing you do could have a big effect. Look what happened to Arlo.

ARLO'S STORY

Arlo saw a TV show about polar bears that really upset him. It showed pictures of polar bears literally starving to death because the ice they hunt on is disappearing through global warming.

Arlo didn't know what global warming was, so he looked online. He found out about meat farming helping to cause climate change and discovered there was something called Meat-Free Monday.

He told his mum and dad he didn't want to eat meat for his tea on Mondays and when he explained why, they said they would join in.

His dad said, 'Why not see if your school can do meat-free Monday dinners too?'

So Arlo asked his teacher, and she thought it was a great idea.

That meant Arlo's decision to cut his carbon footprint soon spread to a whole family and then a whole school.

Not bad, for one boy!

That's what Arlo did to cut his carbon footprint. He did it because he felt upset about the polar bears. Knowledge is power, but so is emotion.

Imagining what global warming means to people and creatures in other parts of the world, feeling it as well as knowing about it, will help you want to do something about it.

YOU CAN DO IT!
Have a trip to a tropical island

Not really, because it costs too much and you're probably busy at the moment – besides, this chapter's all about cutting your carbon footprint!

Imagine you're lying in a hammock beside a sugar-white beach on a beautiful island. The palm trees are waving gently in a warm tropical breeze. The blue sea is lapping softly on the sand.

Close your eyes, and really imagine it. Feel the warm breeze on your bare arms. Feel the hammock swaying. Taste the salty sea air on your lips. Hear the soft sounds of the water and the palm fronds high above you. Take your time. Enjoy it!

Now imagine a massive storm is coming. The sky is suddenly dark with clouds, the wind is whipping up. As you run for shelter, the palm trees around you are being ripped up by their roots and the sea is surging up the beach in enormous waves.

The cabins and houses along the shore are being torn apart and blown away. People are running and screaming. Where can you go? How can you survive?

When the storm has gone, look round at what is left behind.

We may not have terrible experiences like this in the places we live but we can help to protect people in other parts the world from having them if we cut our carbon footprint.

There's a simple formula for cutting both your carbon footprint and your plastic one: reduce, re-use, recycle.

6

REDUCE, REUSE, RECYCLE

One of the things that make our plastic and carbon footprints bigger is that most of us simply have too much stuff. Adverts tell us all the time, 'You need to buy this - it'll make you feel happy!'

But although buying stuff can make you happy, it definitely doesn't do the same thing for the planet.

Everything that's made in a factory has used fuel and caused pollution, and when we buy something new only to throw it in the rubbish later, it just goes on causing pollution.

Rubbish doesn't disappear when the collection lorries come. Most of it ends up in landfill, which means it's tipped into massive great holes that get covered up with earth when they're full.

'That sounds nice and tidy,' I hear you say. 'Out of sight, out of mind!'

Q Do you know any jokes about landfill?
A Yes, but they're all rubbish!

But rubbish in landfill sites produces two nasty greenhouse gases, carbon dioxide and methane. Methane is flammable, and landfill sites can collect some of it and burn it off, but that process also releases poisonous chemicals into the atmosphere.

Besides greenhouse gases, rubbish in landfill produces a revolting black liquid called 'leachate' that's full of toxic chemicals that can seep down into rivers and groundwater.

And there's more! Landfill sites use up lots of land and, even when they're full and covered up with soil, that land can't be used again for years and years. It has to be checked for toxic chemicals until it's clean enough to use for other things like parks and golf courses, but it can't be used to build houses on.

One alternative to landfill is burning rubbish to generate electricity, but that produces higher carbon emissions than coal-fired power stations.

Whichever way we try to dispose of our rubbish, by burying it in landfill or burning it in incinerators, it always has to be transported in heavy lorries that run on fossil fuels and add to air pollution.

Stuff is great - we just use too much of it. So here are three ways to start using less: reduce, reuse and recycle.

REDUCE, REUSE, RECYCLE!

Isn't it funny how there always seem to be three R's? In education, there's reading, riting, rithmetic (yes, I know – whoever thought of that one really should go back to school!). You can read about three more R's - rules, rights, responsibilities - in *70 Ways to Boost Your Self-Esteem*. (It's by me and it's really good!)

So now let's look at the three R's of having a green day.

1 REDUCE MEANS DON'T BUY SO MUCH NEW STUFF

This is far and away the best of the three because, if you haven't bought something in the first place, there's nothing that's had to be manufactured or transported and there's nothing that will have to be recycled or reused.

Not buying new stuff is a whole lot cheaper too ☺

YOU CAN DO IT!
Make a fancy dress box

Fancy dress is one of the things we buy to just use once or twice, at Halloween, for example. Instead of buying ready-made costumes, start collecting interesting clothes and hats from jumble sales. carboots or charity shops so that any time you need a costume, you can make up your own.

YOU CAN DO IT!
Swap for a day

If you sometimes get bored of wearing the same old things, why not do a swap for a day with one of your friends? Obviously, you need to do it with someone who's roughly the same size!

I'm not saying you should never buy a single nother lovely new thing for the rest of your life – I'm just saying, ask yourself before you buy, 'Do I really want this? Do I really need it?'

Ask yourself also, 'Do I need to own it?' Could you borrow it from someone else?

Cutting your plastic and carbon footprints isn't about learning to float along like an airy angel and having no footprints at all – it's just about treading more lightly.

Everyone likes getting new things, but we don't have to have every single new thing we want.

YOU CAN DO IT!
Press pause

When you see something you want, press pause. Quite often, if you don't buy it straight away, it won't feel at all important in a day or two.

2 REUSE MEANS EITHER FIND A DIFFERENT USE FOR OLD STUFF OR GIVE IT TO SOMEONE ELSE, SO THEY CAN USE IT AFTER YOU

Before you send things to the dump or recycling plant, see if you can find another use for them. Maybe a mug with the handle missing could make a nice pot for your pens and pencils. Maybe you could use the pictures from old magazines to make a collage for your bedroom wall.

If you can't find another use for your old things but they aren't broken, give them to a charity shop, car boot or jumble sale for someone else to use.

YOU CAN DO IT!
Give something away

Give something you don't need any more to a charity shop or jumble sale.

While you're at it, ask the rest of the family if they've got anything they don't need, and take that too.

If you've got things that are broken but you still need them, see if someone can mend them for you. Reusing also means repairing things that can be repaired, instead of just throwing them away.

YOU CAN DO IT!
Learn to sew

Ask your mum/dad/grandpa/nan/big bro or whoever in your family knows how to sew if they can teach you to do it too. Learning how to sew on a button is a start.

Learning to sew means you'll be able to make new things from your old clothes, or from other people's old clothes you've found in charity shops.

You can make great cushion covers out of old shirts and skirts, for example.

YOU CAN DO IT!
Learn to knit

While you're at it, find out if anyone among your family or friends knows how to knit. You only need to learn one or two kinds of stitch and you can make a whole jumper. How cool is that?

3 RECYCLE MEANS MAKE OLD STUFF INTO SOMETHING NEW

For example, recycled glass bottles can be made into new glass bottles and drinking glasses or used in different products such as bricks. Recycled plastic bottles can be made into new plastic bottles, or a range of completely different products such as fleeces.

YOUNG ECO WARRIOR – USA
Maya Penn – making new clothes from old

Maya Penn started her sustainable accessories business, Maya's Ideas, when she was just eight years old, using material from old clothes along with organic, sustainably grown natural fabrics.

Ten years later, she has won many awards and works as an adviser to big fashion brands, helping them to make their businesses more eco-friendly.

A lot of products carry a symbol that shows they can be recycled. The most common ones include an arrow going round in a circle and a green square.

YOU CAN DO IT!
Spot your recyclables

Lots of things can't be recycled – such as tissues, plastic toys, drinking glasses, mirrors, wet wipes, dirty pizza boxes, unwashed food jars, crisp and sweet packets, cotton wool, toothpaste tubes and cling film. But lots of things can. It partly depends on where you live.

Search online to see what can be recycled in your area. Find a felt tip or marking pen.

Go through the products in your bathroom, kitchen, living room and bedroom that normally go in the trash when they're empty, and put a big dot or cross on everything that can go in the recycling.

The reason a lot of things that could be recycled don't get recycled is because it takes time to work out exactly which ones can. If your mum/dad/carer has got too much else on their to-do list, they might be really pleased if you could do it for them.

TIP: You only need to mark things a few times because before long it just becomes automatic to recycle things you've recycled before. 'Empty shampoo bottle – oh yes, that goes in the recycling!'

Here are some more fascinating facts about recycling:

- When aluminium drinks cans are recycled, they can be made into new cans, filled up and back in the shops in just six weeks.
- Steel can be recycled over and over again into all sorts of different things.
- Zinc from old mobile phones can be used in shipbuilding.
- Gold found in games consoles can be made into jewelry.
- The average family uses six trees worth of paper each year.
- Five out of six glass bottles are thrown away.
- All glass can be recycled but glass that is just thrown away will never decompose.
- Unwanted electrical things like toasters and TVs are taken apart at a reprocessing plant where they are shredded into small pieces to be recycled.
- Recycled paper produces 73% less air pollution than paper made from raw materials.

It's always better to recycle things than just throw them away, but not everything can be recycled, and the process of recycling takes transportation and electricity, so it does cause some pollution.

The three R's of planet saving aren't complicated. The best one is the first – reduce. It's the most straightforward too. What could be simpler than just cutting the amount of stuff you buy?

Do the 'Reuse and recycle puzzle' to see if you've got the hang of the other two. It's fully reusable because when you've done it you can get your friends to do it too!

THE RECYCLE AND REUSE PUZZLE

You've tidied up your bedroom and now you've got to puzzle out what to do with all the stuff you don't need any more.

See if you can put everything in the right bin.

ALL DONE? HOW DID YOU DO?

The odd sock, broken pencil case, used tissue and empty juice carton all need to go in the rubbish.

The lemonade can, throat sweets box and till receipt can go in the recycling.

The hat you hate, jigsaw and the tee shirt that's too small can go in the charity shop box... unless you've got a little sis who likes jigsaws or you're planning to turn the tee shirt into a cushion cover, of course.

The three R's – reduce, reuse and recycle - are the key to cutting those mucky carbon and plastic footprints so that humans and animals can go on having a lovely world to live in, instead of a gigantic rubbish tip.

Having new stuff might be fun and make you feel good, but so does breathing clean air and not having to pick your way through piles of litter.

Thinking about reducing, reusing and recycling things means that instead of just throwing things away, we ask ourselves, 'What else could I use this for?' and 'Who else might find a use for it?' and instead of just buying something new we ask, 'Could I do a swap? Could I make it myself? Could I mend something I've already got?'

That's a much more creative way of living and being more creative makes us feel happy. That's a scientific fact!

YOU CAN DO IT!
Get creative

Make a birthday/Christmas/ Mother's Day/ Father's Day/ thank you/ get well card. Cut the back off an old cereal or tissues box and fold it, printed side out.

Stick pictures from old magazines all over the printed surface. If you haven't got any magazines, see what else you can find – scraps of wrapping paper, maps or leaflets could look good, or even pictures from some used packaging. If it isn't in the recycling bag, you'd better ask first!

Then get really creative and see if you can work out how to make an envelope too.

Giving what we don't want any more to charity shops and swapping with our friends, making new things out of old ones and sorting our recycling is a much more community-minded way of living than just buying things and throwing them away.

So when we nurture nature, we nurture each other too. Group hug!

7

GO GREEN TOGETHER

When you start wanting to do your bit for the planet, it can feel like everyone else should start doing it too. But there's no point getting angry or preachy – simply making small changes in the way you do things will have an effect on the other people around you.

'Small pebbles make big ripples,' as they say, and that reminds me of little Rosie, who made a decision for herself that changed her whole family.

LITTLE ROSIE'S STORY

When Rosie was about four, she and her family went to her grandparents' house for Christmas dinner.

Grannie asked Rosie, 'Would you like some chicken, or just a sausage?'

93

Rosie had just got a pet chicken. She looked at the chicken on the big serving dish and said, 'Isn't it funny? Chicken looks just like a real chicken. It's the same size and shape!'

All the grown-ups laughed. 'That's because it **is** a real chicken!'

Rosie was shocked. 'I don't want to eat a real chicken,' she sobbed.

Rosie had eaten chicken before, but she had just thought of it as meat, not a living creature that had been killed. As soon as she saw it that way, she chose not to eat it.

When Rosie's mum and dad saw how she felt, they felt it too. From then on, the whole family stopped eating meat and chose to become vegetarian.

Little Rosie changed her whole family without trying to make them change at all. So did the little litter picker I told you about in Chapter Three, who started picking up litter because she saw someone throw rubbish out of their car window.

The little litter picker didn't say 'Everyone should stop chucking litter out of their cars!' – she didn't march up and down with a banner. She said, 'If people see me picking up litter from my road, maybe it'll make them think twice before they throw rubbish out of their car next time.'

It almost always works best to decide what you want to

do and let other people decide for themselves whether they want to do it too.

Trying to force your opinion on other people doesn't usually work, because it sets up a reaction.

'YOU HAVE TO THINK THIS AND DO THAT!'

'NO I DON'T!'

If you try to get people to think and behave the way you do by being pushy, preachy or naggy, you'll probably send them running for a bag of crisps and a bottle of cola.

That's psychology! See if you understand psychology with this 'Can you make them see green?' psychology quiz.

THE 'CAN YOU MAKE THEM SEE GREEN?' QUIZ

1. Your dad says there's no point worrying about the planet because one person can't make a difference. Do you
   a. Tell him he's wrong – and then go on and on about it.
   b. Explain that you want to do your bit because that feels better than not trying to do anything at all.
2. Your mum can't stand moths – they give her the creeps, so if she sees one she hoovers it up. Do you
   a. Hide the hoover.
   b. Offer to catch the moth, if she sees one, and put it outside.

3. Your mate chucks her empty crisp packet in the gutter. Do you
   a. Shout at her and try to make her pick it up.
   b. Pick it up and put it in the bin.
4. Your big sis is sprawled on the sofa doing her nails, with the curtains shut and the lights on, though it's broad daylight outside. Do you
   a. Tell her she's killing the planet, fling back the curtains and switch off the light.
   b. Suggest it might be easier to see what she's doing with the curtains open.
5. Your little bro doesn't want your hand-me-down jumper. Do you
   a. Laugh and say, 'Worst luck!'
   b. Tell him you loved that jumper and you're glad it's not getting thrown away.

ANSWERS.

IF YOU GOT ANY A'S... Stop that right now – you're making them see red!

IF YOU GOT B'S... Full steam ahead – you're helping them see green.

96

You can't force your family and friends to go green with you, but they might gradually start turning green when they notice what you're doing. If they don't, that still doesn't mean you have to do it all on your own.

YOU ARE NOT ALONE!

As soon as you start trying to do your bit for the planet, you'll begin to notice there are lots of other people doing the same. There will be events in your area for children and families who want to get out and help nature, organised by local conservation groups.

YOU CAN DO IT!
Find your nearest nature club

Search online for your nearest nature club for kids.
 For example, in the UK, there are lots of activities organised by the Wildlife Trusts http://www.wildlifetrusts. org/natureclubs and The Royal Society for the Protection of Birds https://www.rspb.org.uk/fun-and-learning/for-families/family-wild-challenge/what-is-wild-challenge
 A quick search will turn up litter picks, beach cleans, beekeeper days, mini beast safaris – all sorts of activities going on near you in woodlands or city parks, countryside or beaches.

Q Why was the sand wet?
A Because the sea weed!

Joining groups that care about the natural world isn't only encouraging and fun – it's also a great way of getting ideas for how you could set up your own group activities.

The key to success is that it has to be fun. People will come along because they want to, not because you've twisted their arm!

YOU CAN DO IT!
Join in with a local litter pick – or have your own

If you search online 'litter pick' plus your area, you'll probably find quite a few. If you happen to live near the coast, you could search 'beach clean' plus your area instead.

If you can't find one to join in with, see if your mum/dad/bro/sis/grandpa/gran/mates would like to get together and do a litter pick in the streets near you, or ask your teacher if you can organise one at school.

You can make it more fun by having a competition to see who can find the weirdest bit of litter. You'd be surprised what people throw away!

YOU CAN DO IT!
Build the best bug hotel

Building a bug hotel was one of the ideas in the chapter about looking after little animals. It's fun to do on your own, but even better to do with family or friends. So see if anyone would like to have a best bug hotel competition.

Build your bug hotels, leave them for a week or two, then see who has managed to attract the most bugs.

YOU CAN DO IT!
Have a tallest sunflower competition

Everyone loves sunflowers because they're so big and bright, and everyone loves a competition! All you need is a packet of seeds and a patch of ground.

Share the seeds out between everyone who is taking part. Follow the instructions on the packet – and you're off!

NOTE: If you haven't got a patch of ground at home or at school, you can grow your sunflowers in a pot.

ANOTHER NOTE: When the flowers die, as the petals begin to wither, the seeds in the middle will ripen. If you leave them until they're starting to come loose, then cut the sunflower from the stem and brush the seeds off with your hand, you can keep them to plant next year.

YET ANOTHER NOTE: If you like, you can leave the sunflowers outside and wait for the birds to come and get the seeds. Then you'll be looking after little creatures too.

BE A BLUE TIT, NOT A BOSSY BOOTS

In the old days when milkmen left glass bottles of milk on the doorstep, blue tits used to peck through the foil tops to get to the milk. How did they know to do that? One of them discovered it by chance and told all his mates.

Then each of them told other blue tits, because that's the nature of blue tits – they love to share the good stuff. If a robin had found out how to peck through the foil to the milk, he'd probably have kept it to himself!

If helping to care for nature makes you feel good and you want to share the good stuff, that's the best way of getting other people to care for nature too. Much better than nagging and criticising.

Sean found a clever way of turning his nan green, without her even noticing!

SEAN'S STORY

Sean's nan lived in a neighbourhood that had an open gardens day every summer. She loved taking part, opening her garden for her neighbours to visit and enjoy, and making lots of tea and cakes to raise money for Cancer Research (Sean's grandpa died of cancer before Sean was born).

Sean asked his nan if he could set up a swaps table by the gate, where people could leave any old stuff they didn't want any more, and take away different stuff for free.

Sean's nan put a notice on her gate a few weeks before the day, so that people would know to bring their swaps, and everyone did.

The swaps table was so popular, Sean's nan decided to have one every month through the year. It wasn't open gardens, but she still made tea and cakes to sell for Cancer Research, just for the stuff-swappers who came.

When Sean couldn't help out any more because he had exams, his nan's friends helped out instead. One of them, visiting from a different town, liked the idea so much she set up a stuff swap in her road as well.

That's lots of stuff getting reused, and lots of people having fun!

One person doing their bit to save the planet will make a difference, and not just in terms of the plastic bag they don't use or the light they switch off. They'll make a difference because we're social animals – what we do has an effect on the people around us, and we like to do things together.

YOU CAN DO IT!
Put Earth Hour on your calendar

Every year, the WWF (World Wide Fund for Nature) sets
the date and time for Earth Hour, when people all over the
world switch off the lights to show that they care about our
planet's future.

Hundreds of millions of people join in – nearly ten
million in the UK alone – and the lights are even switched
off in big public buildings like the Sydney Opera House,
the Eiffel Tower and Buckingham Palace.

Check out the https://www.earthhour.org website
to find out when the next one is. Put the date in your
calendar. Tell your friends, and maybe start planning how
you might celebrate Earth Hour together.

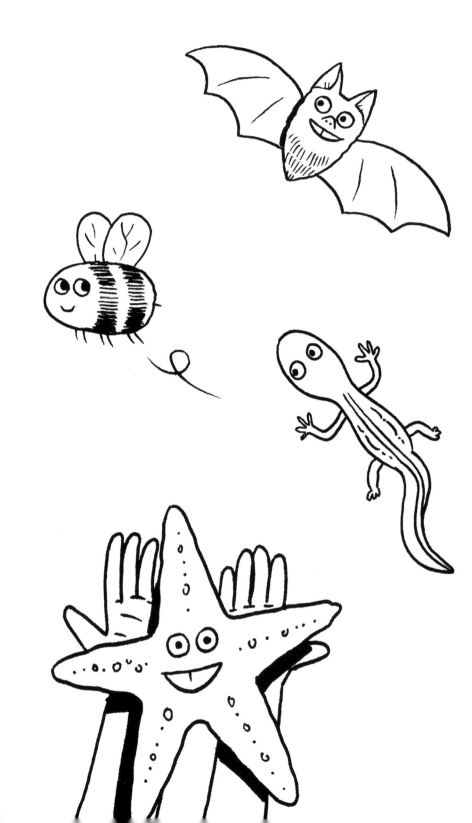

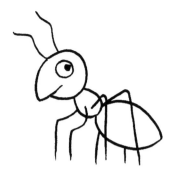

8

ENJOY!

On a scale of 1-100, how amazing are the following?

1. A bird ▦
2. An tree ▦
3. A bumble bee ▦
4. A horse ▦
5. An iceberg ▦
6. You ▦
7. A shark ▦
8. A stinging nettle ▦
9. A toad ▦
10. The ocean ▦

ANSWERS: They're all 100% amazing!

We tend to take the natural world for granted, and not even notice it. But when you look – when you really look – you can't help realising that every single thing in nature is a miracle.

It's up to us what happens to our planet. We've been turning it into a rubbish tip, with dirty seas, dirty air and dirty land because we didn't understand the harm we were doing.

Now we do understand. Our way of living means the climate is changing, whole species are disappearing, and we're creating dead zones that can't support any kind of life at all.

But knowledge is power, and now that we understand there's a problem, we can start doing something about it.

The great thing is that once we accept we have to change, there's a lot to enjoy about looking after nature.

THE JOY OF AWARENESS

As soon as you start to think about how you can help the planet you become heaps more aware of how beautiful it is, and there's joy in just noticing.

AALIYAH'S STORY - PART ONE

Aaliyah was sitting on the grass with her mum when a ladybird landed on her hand. She was going to flick it off but her mum said, 'Don't do that. It's lucky when a ladybird lands on you!'

'Why is it lucky?' asked Aaliyah. Her mum shrugged. 'I don't know. It's just what people say.'

They looked down at the ladybird. It had six legs and seven spots, three on each side and one in the middle. When it opened the red shiny sides of its shell, they could see the tiny black wings underneath. But it didn't fly away. Instead, it let out a little drop of yellow liquid and dropped down dead.

At least, that's what Aaliyah thought had happened but then, to her astonishment, the ladybird suddenly perked up and flew away.

109

YOU CAN DO IT!
Do some cloud watching

There are ten different types of cloud and they all make shapes in the sky. Sometimes they move and change shape quite fast, sometimes more slowly.

On a day when the sky is mostly blue, take some time to watch the clouds. Imagine they are moving pictures. What do they look like? One might remind you of a cupcake, another could be a big yacht sailing across the sky.

NOTE: Cloud-watching is nice with your mum/dad/gran/grandpa/cousin/mates, because everyone sees different things in the shapes of clouds.

THE JOY OF LEARNING

When you start to notice nature, you feel curious, and curiosity leads to the best kind of learning. It's much easier and more fun to learn things you want to know than things other people say you ought to.

Q What animals do you have to watch out for in exams?
A Cheetahs

AALIYAH'S STORY - PART TWO

After the ladybird had flown away, Aaliyah wiped the yellow stuff off her hand with a leaf. 'Is that its blood?' she asked her mum. 'Why is its blood yellow?'

'Let's find out!' said her mum, taking out her phone.

They found out that the yellow stuff wasn't ladybirds' blood, but something they secreted from their knees if they felt threatened; they secreted the yellow stuff and then played dead. Aaliyah had certainly fallen for it!

Aaliyah and her mum found out lots of other things while they were looking, such as that ladybirds are called ladybugs in America and lady beetles in Europe. They discovered that not all ladybirds are red, not all ladybirds' spots are black and not all ladybirds have seven.

They read that ladybirds are considered lucky in lots of different cultures, probably because they protect food crops by eating greenfly and other insects that gobble up plants. A ladybird can eat 40 or 50 greenfly in one day, which is pretty impressive considering how small a ladybird is.

'They love plants like geraniums and old logs with loose bark because those can be full of tiny insects,' read Aaliyah, scrolling down. She was getting an idea...

Nature is HUGE, so there's no end to what you can learn. I've learnt some great things while I've been writing this book, such as:

- Trees communicate with each other by sending chemical messages through an underground network of fungi that grow around and inside their roots.
- Crows are really clever – they can use tools. That's something scientists used to think only humans and monkeys could do.
- Octopuses are aliens – well, they might be! Some researchers think they could have evolved from squid because of a space virus brought in when a comet crashed into the earth.

10 WEIRD AND WONDERFUL OCTOPUS FACTS

1. Octopuses have three hearts, and one of them stops beating when they swim.
2. They can squirt a kind of ink that makes predators lose their sight and sense of smell for a while.
3. They can see with their skin.
4. They can completely change colour in under a second.
5. They don't just change colour – they can change the texture of their skin so they look like a piece of rock or seaweed.
6. They have blue blood.
7. An octopus bite can paralyse a human being in minutes.

8. Two thirds of an octopus's brain is in its arms.
9. An octopus's brain has as many neurons as a dog or a three year-old child.
10. A famous octopus named Paul correctly predicted the results of 12 out of 14 football matches played by the German national team. He's got his own Wikipedia page!

THE JOY OF FEELING CONNECTED

The joy of awareness leads to curiosity; that leads to learning, and then learning leads to another joy, the joy of feeling connected – because the more we learn about the planet the clearer it becomes that everything in nature is connected.

Humans and animals need oxygen to survive – we get it from the air when we breathe in and release carbon dioxide into the air when we breathe out. Where does the oxygen come from? Where does the carbon dioxide go?

Plants need carbon dioxide to make their food, and they release oxygen in the process. So the animals need the plants and the plants need the animals to survive.

The whole earth is like a single being, breathing in and breathing out, and every plant and animal plays its part.

YOU CAN DO IT!
Hug a tree

It's a scientific fact that hugging trees is good for you – yes, really! Research shows that hanging around with trees improves all sorts of conditions such as sadness, stress, headaches and poor concentration. You can try it for yourself.

Obviously, you might want to be a bit subtle about it, because not everyone knows about the health benefits of tree hugging and a lot of people might think it's just plain weird.

Choose a tree near your home – in your garden maybe, or your local park – so you can easily visit it again. Touch it with the palms of your hands. Lean your back against it. Talk to it.

Give your tree a hug. Imagine it taking away all your worries and recycling them through the earth, giving you back the strength and stability you need, in just the same way as trees take the carbon dioxide we don't need and give back the oxygen we do.

Let your tree be a role model, showing you how to stand tall and stay rooted even in the stormiest times. Before you go, say thank you to your tree for helping you feel better.

TREE HUGGING NOTE: You don't have to stick to one tree. Trees are all different, like humans, and you might find you like different ones when you're in different moods.

YOU CAN DO IT!
Breathe!

Have you noticed lately that you're breathing? Notice now.

Breathe in to a count of six, feeling grateful for all the lovely oxygen the plants and trees have given you.

Breathe out to a count of six, imagining you are giving your carbon dioxide to the plants and trees.

One of the problems with modern living is it's easy to lose that sense of connection with the natural world. Some psychologists say that in the evolution of our species, we've only lived on concrete and tarmac for a tiny amount of time, and we still need to feel the earth beneath our feet for our emotional wellbeing. Their prescription for difficult feelings is simply to get out in nature.

Whenever you can, get out in the open air. Walk instead of taking the bus, play games, do sports, eat your lunch out of doors. Being in nature isn't just great for your physical body, it can help you stay calm and balanced emotionally too.

YOU CAN DO IT!
Play outside

You're never too old to play outside and there are loads of games you can play that don't need special equipment, such as:

- Running races and long jump competitions
- Skimming stones and target practice, throwing pebbles at an empty can
- Games of chase, such as 'it', 'shipwrecked' or 'stuck-in-the-mud'

Even ones that do need equipment don't need very much. French cricket and rounders just need a bat and ball, and football doesn't even need the bat!

PLAYING OUTSIDE NOTE: Remember you can always improvise. I've played many a game of French cricket on the beach with a bit of driftwood for a bat and a pair of rolled-up socks for a ball, or footie at the park using sweaters for goal posts. Be creative!

ANOTHER NOTE: There are lots of outdoors games and variations. Ask your friends what outdoor games they know – learn new ones. Ask your parents, aunties and uncles and grandparents too – they might love teaching you the games they used to play when they were at school.

YOU CAN DO IT!
Have a picnic

If you can't get your school/youth group/family to have a big picnic in a local park or open space, just get together with a few mates. Your picnic doesn't have to be anywhere wild – the local park or garden will do fine – but you obviously don't want it to include anything wrapped in single-use plastic.

A single-use-plastic free picnic is a great way of enjoying nature and protecting it, all at the same time!

If it isn't easy getting out into nature more, think about bringing nature inside too.

THE JOY OF HELPING

When we see we're all connected then we see that we all matter. Everyone can contribute. We can all help our planet by making greener choices, and happiness experts say helping others is a powerful happiness booster.

AALIYAH'S STORY - PART THREE

Aaliyah wasn't sure what nasturtiums looked like, but she knew that ladybirds loved them so she asked her mum. 'Grandpa's got some in his garden,' Aaliyah's mum said. 'Why?'

'I'm going to make a ladybird heaven,' said Aaliyah.

Aaliyah's grandpa gave her a nasturtium in a pot and a few logs from his wood pile. She noticed the underside of the nasturtium leaves had clusters of greenfly on them and there were little insects crawling around under the loose bark on the logs.

When Aaliyah got home, she put the nasturtium beside the back door step and arranged the logs around it.

Her mum was worried she might be disappointed if no ladybirds came... but by then, Aaliyah was busy finding out fascinating facts about greenflies!

Did you know that greenflies' poo is a kind of sugar? (It's called 'honeydew.')

The key to enjoying helping is not to beat yourself up about all the things you don't do, that you know you could, but focus on the things you do manage to do. Every little helps, and a little bit is better than nothing at all.

YOU CAN DO IT!
Give yourself a pat on the back

Be proud of yourself for every little thing you do to help the planet. You learnt about the problems of global warming and pollution – well done, you!

You didn't flush your plaster down the loo... you took your old lego to the charity shop... you grew a pot of bee-friendly flowers...

Well done, well done, you!

THE GREATEST JOY OF ALL

Everyone knows that the greatest joy of all is love. Check it out right now. Think of someone or something you love – your gran or grandpa, say, or playing football.

Take a few minutes over it. Notice what happens in your body – how your breathing changes and your muscles soften and relax. Notice your face as well – are you smiling?

That's what this book is all about – loving the amazing world we live in and doing what we can to help look after it.

YOUR 'HOW I'VE MADE A DIFFERENCE' LIST

The brilliant thing is that every little change you make soon becomes a habit, so you don't even have to think about unplugging your phone when it's fully charged or putting your used tissues in the bin instead of down the toilet – you just do it.

And you only have to do some of the things in this book once, in order to start changing the whole way you think about yourself and the world.

Here's a handy tick list so you can keep a record of all the things you've done.

OTHER BOOKS BY JENNY ALEXANDER

BULLIES, BIGMOUTHS AND SO-CALLED FRIENDS

This book doesn't just show you how to pretend you don't care – it shows you how to really not care – so you can get on with your own life and not let someone else's lack of social skills (that's putting it nicely!) spoil everything. Plus it's got lots of quizzes and cartoons and stuff, so it's a great read.

'No other author has done the job on the subject of bullying as well as Alexander does'
JUNIOR MAGAZINE

HOW 2B HAPPY

Everyone gets down in the dumps sometimes – it's only natural – but this book shows you how to bounce back quicker and develop a happy lifestyle. Plus it's got lots of quizzes, cartoons, stories and jokes

10 WAYS TO BOOST YOUR SELF-ESTEEM

Anyone's self-esteem can take a knock sometimes
and you can use this book to build yourself back up
any time you need a boost. It's got jokes, quizzes,
real-life stories and fun things to do to help you
feel confident and glad that you're you.

10 WAYS TO BULLY-PROOF YOURSELF

Bullying can make you feel helpless, scared,
angry and unhappy. It can make you want to crawl
under the covers and never come out again. But
if you do that, the bullies win. Don't let them!

You can learn to bully-proof yourself
– this book will show you how.

GOING UP! THE NO-WORRIES GUIDE TO SECONDARY SCHOOL

Worries are a normal part of every new adventure – they're nature's way of making you prepare. One way of preparing is by getting information – and all the information you need about going up to secondary school is right here!

'The author knows what makes Y6 laugh
– the jokes are really good!'
BEN AMBERLEY-SMITH, 11, QUOTED IN THE TEACHER

HOW TO BE A BRILLIANT WRITER

Not as in, how to get great SAT results, but as in how to make writing a brilliant part of your everyday life (though actually doing lots of writing for fun means your SAT results will get better all on their own).

'An essential guide for young, aspiring writers'
HEADTEACHER UPDATE

HOW TO GET WHAT YOU WANT
BY PEONY PINKER

If you like funny stories about families, pets and friends, you'll love reading the Peony Pinker books – and you'll pick up lots of useful tips along the way!

As well as 'How to get what you want, by Peony Pinker', you can read 'How to get the friends you want', 'How to get the family you want' and 'How to get the body you want', all by Peony Pinker, too.

'Entertaining and humorous... if you have readers looking for an alternative to Jacqueline Wilson, then introduce them to Peony'
THE SCHOOL LIBRARIAN

Printed in Great Britain
by Amazon